Gabby

Joyce Grant

Illustrated by

Jan Dolby

Fitzhenry & Whiteside

Text copyright © 2013 Joyce Grant
Illustrations copyright © 2013 Jan Dolby

Published in Canada by Fitzhenry & Whiteside, 195 Allstate Parkway, Markham, Ontario L3R 4T8

Published in the United States in 2013 by Fitzhenry & Whiteside, 311 Washington Street, Brighton, Massachusetts 02135

www.fitzhenry.ca   godwit@fitzhenry.ca

10 9 8 7 6 5 4 3 2 1

Library and Archives Canada Cataloguing in Publication
Grant, Joyce, 1963-
Gabby / by Joyce Grant ; illustrations by Jan Dolby.
ISBN 978-1-55455-250-4
I. Dolby, Jan, 1967- II. Title.
PS8613.R3653G33 2012   jC813'.6   C2012-904075-4

Publisher Cataloging-in-Publication Data (U.S.)
Grant, Joyce.
Gabby / Joyce Grant ; illustrated by Jan Dolby.
[32] p. : col.ill. ; cm.
Summary: When a book falls out of a little girl's hands and tumbles to the floor, it sets in motion a chain of funny, dramatic events in this tale about friendship.
ISBN: 978-1-55455-250-4
1. Friendship – Juvenile fiction. I. Dolby, Jan. II. Title.
[E] dc23   PZ7.G7386Ga 2012

Fitzhenry & Whiteside acknowledges with thanks the Canada Council for the Arts, and the Ontario Arts Council for their support of our publishing program. We acknowledge the financial support of the Government of Canada through the Canada Book Fund (CBF) for our publishing activities.

ONTARIO ARTS COUNCIL
CONSEIL DES ARTS DE L'ONTARIO

Canada Council
for the Arts

Conseil des Arts
du Canada

Cover and interior design by Daniel Choi
Cover image by Jan Dolby
Printed in China by Sheck Wah Tong Printing Press Ltd. in October 2012
Job# 63780

For Bennett
—J.G.

For my husband Dave, the biggest kid in my life.
—J.D.

Gabby was almost finished tidying her playroom.

She reached, reached, reached to put her last book away when suddenly...

...the book tumbled out of her hands and hit the shelf — **wham!**

To her surprise, the letters *bounced* right out of the book!

Letters littered her whole playroom.

There was a **c** on the carpet...

...an **a** on her armchair...

...and a **†** on the table.

They made a word.

"Cuh... ah... tuh... **cat**!" said Gabby.

Gabby smiled at the **cat**. The **cat** blinked at Gabby.

"Are you hungry?" she asked the **cat**.

"*Meow!*" he answered and licked her hand.

But what could Gabby give the **cat** to eat?

She looked around her playroom and found...

...an i in her ice-cream bowl,

...an s on the sofa,

...an f on the floor,

...and a teeny, tiny h that was stuck right in her hair.

"Fish!" she said happily, and suddenly there was a yummy fish for her new friend to eat.

As the **cat** enjoyed his meal, Gabby noticed a suspicious heap of letters in the corner...

...a **b** beside the broom,

an **i** inside her ice skate,

an **r** on the rug,

and a **d** near the door.

"Oh no!" she cried, "That spells...

The **bird** spied the **cat**.

The **cat** glared at the **bird**.

The **cat** hissed and leapt at the **bird**.

The **bird** flapped her wings in a panic, sending feathers flying.

Gabby would have to act fast.

But what could she do?

Then Gabby had a brilliant idea!

She grabbed an f, an r, and an i...

...then she gathered e, n, d, and s.

She put all the letters together near the frightened **bird** and the hissing **cat**.

"Friends!" she cried.

And sure enough, the **cat** relaxed and the **bird** stopped her frantic flapping.

They became **friends**.

Gabby looked around the room again.

She found the biggest, plumpest, warmest looking letters she could find, and formed an enormous pillow.

Then Gabby and her two new friends snuggled down into their cozy reading spot…

...to read another book.

Make your Letters

bounce

Create a collection of about fifty letters.

You can:
- Cut big letters out of some old newspapers, magazines, or flyers.
- Write them on small cue cards or cut-up squares of paper

Make sure that you have at least one of each letter. You will probably want to have 2 or 3 copies of commonly used letters like r, s, t, l, and n. Make sure you have lots of vowels.
Once you have about 40 or 50 letters, put them in a folder.
Then open the folder and...throw the letters into the air! Watch them scatter around the room!
Look at the letters around the room. Can you see any words? Gather a few letters together to make whatever words you can find.

Bonus activity: Try making several words or even a sentence!

A, E, I, O, U (and sometimes Y) are vowels. All the other letters in the alphabet are called consonants

Fun Gabby Activities–*For You!*

Memory Game
(by yourself or with a friend or two!)

- Go to Gabby's website at **www.fitzhenry.ca/Gabby** to find printable Memory Game sheets or make your own letter cards.
- Print out the UPPER CASE and **lower case** letter sheets. (Hint: For an easier version of the game, print each sheet on different coloured paper.)
- Cut out the letter boxes.
- Match each UPPER CASE letter with its **lower case** letter.
- Find the 5 pairs of vowels (a, e, i, o, u) and mix them up.
- Arrange them face down on a desk or table.
- Flip over two rectangles and read the letters on the other side. Do they match? If they do, keep the matching pair. If they don't, flip them over and try two more letters. See if you (and your friends) can find all the matching pairs.

Bonus challenge: Add more letter pairs to the game! Start with 5 pairs of letters (10 letters) and then try 8 or 10—or even all 26 letter pairs!

ABCDEFGHIJKLMNOPQRSTUVWXYZ

Gabby's Ribbon Words

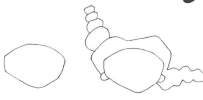

Find the Frog!

Did you notice? There is a little green frog on every page of this book. Go back over the story and see if you can find him.

Bonus activity: Sometimes, the frog is holding a little letter. Starting at the beginning of the story, if you write these letters down on a piece of paper you will discover Gabby's full name.

Gabriella

- Tape together a few strips of paper or use some wide paper ribbon.
- Copy a short sentence from this book onto the strip. Be sure to use a capital letter at the beginning and a period at the end of the sentence.
- Read the sentence out loud.
- Cut the ribbon up so that each word is on a separate strip of paper.
- Mix the words all up.
- Try to put the words back together into a sentence. (Hint: Use the capital letter from the first word and the period after the last word as clues.)

How to Draw Gabby

Draw an oval.   Add hair.   Add nose, eyes and mouth.   Add a flower. Add dots to eyes and swirls on her hair.

How to Draw the Cat

Draw the head.   Add eyes and nose.   Add dots to eyes. Add mouth and whiskers.

abcdefghijklmnopqrstuvwxyz